Disney PRINCESS

How to Be a Princess

For my parents,
who taught me to believe
in happily ever after
—C.B.C.

ISBN 978-0-7364-3415-7

randomhousekids.com

Cover design by Diana Schoenbrun
Book design by Stephanie Sumulong

Printed in the United States of America

10 9 8 7 6 5 4 3 2

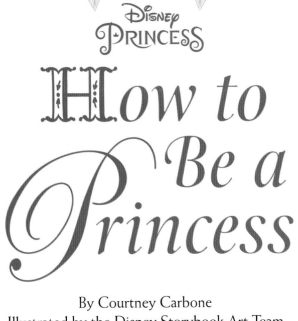

DISNEY PRINCESS

How to Be a Princess

By Courtney Carbone

Illustrated by the Disney Storybook Art Team

Random House 🏠 New York

Contents

Introduction

Some people think that being a princess means having a king and a queen as parents, living in a fancy castle, and having lots of beautiful clothing and treasures. But the Disney Princesses know that what is on the outside doesn't matter nearly as much as what's in your heart.

Being a princess is all about doing the right thing, being loyal to your family and friends, and following your dreams. Discover ways that you can be just like a Disney Princess in your own life!

Meet the Princesses

Jasmine

Independent
and
Smart

Cinderella

Courageous
and
Kind

Tiana

Creative
and
Hardworking

Merida

Adventurous
and
Brave

Rapunzel
Playful and Daring

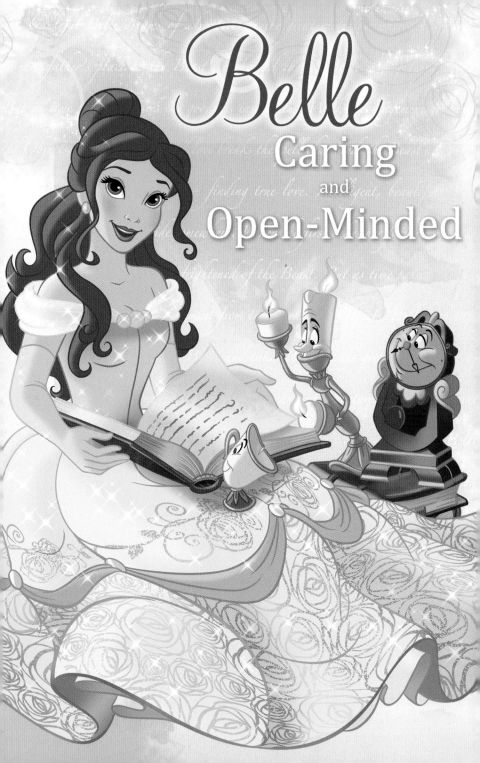

Belle
Caring
and
Open-Minded

Ariel

Friendly and Curious

Pocahontas

Fearless
and
Spirited

Mulan

Loyal
and
Bold

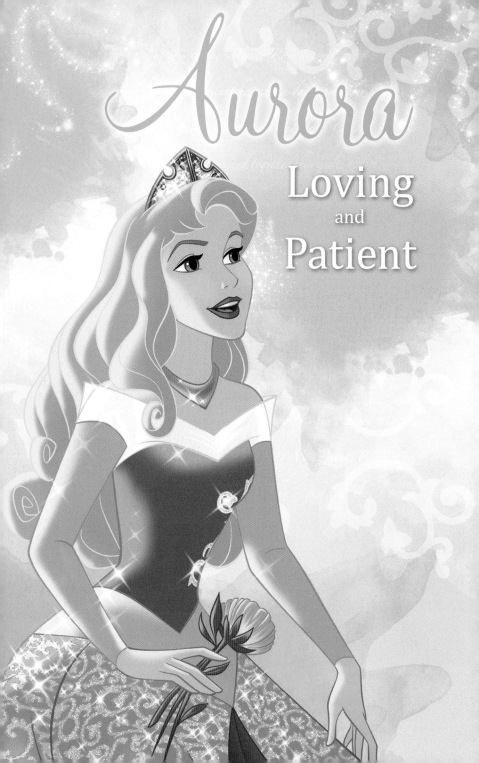

Aurora

Loving
and
Patient

Snow White

Fair and Hopeful

Someone Special

Princesses come in all shapes and sizes, and each one is perfect in her own way—just like you! Because you are a princess-in-training, it's important for you to realize how extraordinary you are, and how you bring a special magic to the world just by being yourself.

How to Feel as Special as a Princess

✦ Always remember that you are one of a kind!

✦ Celebrate the things that make you unique.

✦ Don't compare yourself to others—everyone is different!

✦ Smile every day when you look in the mirror.

✦ Surround yourself with people who love you.

✦ Make a list of all the special things about yourself. Ask your friends to help, and then help them write lists of their own!

Family First

The Disney Princesses come from all different kinds of families. Ariel had a big family with lots of siblings, while Belle and her father had only each other. Cinderella grew up with a stepfamily, and Aurora was raised by the three good fairies. Princesses know that a family is any group of people who love each other.

How to Put Your Family First Like a Princess

✦ Make your family proud by always doing your best!

✦ Treat your family members with love and respect.

✦ Let your parents know what is going on in your life.

✦ Show appreciation for the things others do for you.

✦ Suggest fun new activities to do together—like a weekly board-game night!

✦ Help out with chores around the house.

✦ Keep a list of your family traditions—and start some new ones!

Friends Forever

Tiana loves spending time with her best friend, Charlotte. They play and laugh together, and help make each other's dreams come true. Princesses know it's important to be a good friend, because then others will be good friends to you!

How to Be a Good Friend Like a Princess

✦ Sometimes just being there is the best way to show you care!

✦ Be respectful and polite when you are at a friend's house.

✦ Always keep your promises, whether big or small.

✦ Explore new places and try fun activities together!

✦ Be loyal to your friends.

✦ Admit when you do something wrong, and apologize.

✦ Forgive your friends for their mistakes when they apologize.

✦ Do little things to show you care—like send your friends letters in the mail!

First Impressions

An important thing to remember when you are a princess is to always make a good first impression! This means conducting yourself with confidence and grace. As a princess-in-training, you can practice certain skills that will help you on your royal journey.

How to Act Like a Princess

✦ Introduce yourself and shake hands when you meet new people.

✦ Speak slowly and clearly so others can understand you.

✦ Ask people how they are doing and what is going on in their lives.

✦ Don't interrupt when others are speaking.

✦ Really listen to what people are saying— it's simple but important!

✦ Make eye contact when you are talking to someone.

✦ Remember to be polite and say please and thank you!

Happy & Healthy

Being a princess is more than just fun and games—you have to make taking care of yourself a top priority. A good way to do this is to create an everyday routine that focuses on keeping you happy and healthy!

How to Take Care of Yourself Like a Princess

✦ Brush your teeth every morning and night.

✦ Comb or brush your hair every morning.

✦ Take a shower when your parents tell you to.

✦ Wash your hands carefully throughout the day.

✦ Don't eat too much dessert or junk food.

✦ Do eat lots of fruits and vegetables!

✦ Drink at least eight cups of water every day.

✦ Find a fun exercise or activity to do once a day!

✦ Visit the doctor and dentist regularly.

✦ Get plenty of sleep—which means no dillydallying at bedtime!

Nice & Neat

You might think that being a princess means having a staff of royal butlers and maids to keep things tidy, but the Disney Princesses are actually the ones who keep their castles running smoothly! Part of being a princess means taking pride in caring for your own things.

How to Take Care of
Your Things Like a Princess

+ Make your bed every morning.

+ Put your dirty clothes in the hamper.

+ Hang up wet towels to dry.

+ Keep your things off the floor—you don't want anyone to trip over them!

+ Use small boxes or baskets to store odds and ends.

+ Keep your clothes hung up or folded in neat piles.

+ Give away items you've outgrown or don't need anymore.

+ Keep fragile or valuable items tucked safely away.

Dress to Impress

When you're a princess, you need to look the part! Some princesses, like Cinderella, love dazzling dresses. But others, like Merida, just want to wear comfortable clothes! The good news is you don't need a huge wardrobe to dress like a princess. Dress to impress just by using items you already have!

How to Dress Like a Princess

◆ Remember that a smile is the best accessory!

◆ Wear clothes that fit properly.

◆ Don't be scared to try new patterns or colors.

◆ Wear cute and comfortable shoes—even Cinderella had trouble with high heels!

◆ Keep your clothes clean and wrinkle-free.

◆ Be careful not to rip or stain your clothes.

◆ If someone compliments your look, say thank you!

◆ Think about adding a little sparkle for fancy occasions.

◆ Stand up straight! A princess always has good posture.

◆ Be confident—wear clothes that show your personality!

Princess Parties

When you're a princess, your social calendar is always full of royal balls and celebrations. You might even host a few of your own! But whether they are guests or hostesses, princesses always put their best foot forward and set an example for others to follow.

How to Host a Party Like a Princess

✦ Greet your guests as soon as they arrive.

✦ Be warm and genuine—make sure everyone feels welcome!

✦ Introduce people who do not know each other.

✦ Make sure you have refreshments to serve.

✦ Thank everyone for coming.

How to Attend a Party Like a Princess

✦ RSVP and show up on time.

✦ Bring a gift or a treat to share.

✦ Ask the host if you can help with anything.

✦ Compliment the party venue, refreshments, or decorations.

✦ Thank the host for inviting you.

Mealtime Manners

When Belle ate dinner with the Beast for the first time, she quickly realized that no one had ever taught him table manners! Instead of laughing or teasing him, she tried to make him feel more comfortable. Soon they both had proper table manners!

How to Have Table Manners
Like a Princess

✦ Place your napkin in your lap.

✦ Keep your elbows off the table while you eat.

✦ Eat slowly and take small bites.

✦ Keep your mouth closed while chewing.

✦ Never speak with your mouth full.

✦ Ask others to pass items that are out of reach.

✦ Thank the person who prepared the meal.

✦ Don't be scared to try new foods—you might like them!

✦ Ask to be excused before leaving the table.

✦ Clear your place and offer to help clean up.

Top of the Class

Belle loves reading more than anything! Books are a great way to learn about the world, but there are lots of other ways to become as smart as a princess.

How to Be as Smart as a Princess

+ Read as much as you possibly can, like Belle!

+ Pay attention in school.

+ Write down things you want to remember.

+ Make a comfy study nook where you can do your homework.

+ Don't be afraid to ask questions—that's how you learn!

+ Discuss things you are learning about with family and friends.

+ Watch movies and shows based on true stories.

+ Go to the library to find out about all sorts of topics.

+ Visit museums to learn about art and history.

Princess Pastimes

A princess-in-training needs to stay active! Like Rapunzel, Cinderella, and the rest of the Disney Princesses, you can develop your own special talents by trying new hobbies. You'll never know what you're good at until you try!

How to Keep Busy Like a Princess

✦ Play sports—they're a great way to have fun and stay in shape!

✦ Get creative with an arts and crafts project.

✦ Write a special story in which you are the star!

✦ Decorate, sew, knit, or crochet a piece of clothing.

✦ Design your own jewelry with string, beads, or charms.

✦ Learn how to play a musical instrument. Practice, practice, practice!

✦ Choreograph a fun dance to your favorite song.

✦ Ask an adult to give you a cooking or baking lesson.

✦ Brainstorm a silly play and act it out with friends.

✦ Use a brush as a microphone, and pretend you are a singing sensation!

Adventure Awaits

Part of being a princess means going on exciting adventures! Whether you are taking a Magic Carpet ride like Jasmine or setting sail like Aurora, as a princess-in-training, you'll want to make the most of every special journey!

How to Travel Like a Princess

✦ Read about the history of a place before you visit—this will make the trip more interesting!

✦ Take pictures to capture your memories.

✦ Make a list of all the things you do and see.

✦ Keep mementos like ticket stubs and postcards.

✦ Be open to trying new things and meeting new people!

Brave & Bold

Merida's family wanted her to get married at the Highland Games, but she knew she wasn't ready to settle down. Instead of giving in, Merida followed her own path to happiness. A real princess is always true to her heart!

How to Be as Brave as a Princess

✦ Think for yourself.

✦ Speak up when something doesn't feel right.

✦ Never be shy about what's important to you.

✦ Don't be afraid of things that are different.

✦ Stand up for what you believe in, like Mulan does!

The Power of Peace

Pocahontas knows the importance of patience and understanding. Instead of fearing new visitors who were different, she tried to get to know them better. As a princess-in-training, you should also try to get along with others at school, home, a slumber party—wherever!

How to Get Along with Others Like a Princess

+ Be patient and kind, like Belle.

+ Don't judge people before you get to know them.

+ Listen carefully to how others feel.

+ Offer to share what you have.

+ Focus on what you have in common!

Adorable Animals

Disney Princesses love their fuzzy friends! Some, like Rapunzel, have small, playful pets. Belle and Merida adore their horses. And Aurora loves spending time with forest animals. Princesses always treat all creatures with love and respect.

How to Treat Animals
Like a Princess

✦ Read about animals that interest you.

✦ Offer to help take care of your pets or your friends' pets.

✦ Donate food and supplies to a local animal shelter.

✦ Only feed or pet an animal if an adult tells you it's okay.

✦ Ask your parents if you can set up a bird feeder outside.

✦ Take a trip to the zoo to see all kinds of animals.

✦ Pretend you are Ariel and visit your underwater friends at an aquarium!

✦ Sit in a park and quietly watch animals work and play.

✦ Learn about ways to protect endangered animals.

✦ Make up an imaginary pet that is all your own!

Wonderful World

The first time she left the tower, Rapunzel was surprised to see that there was a whole world outside full of excitement and adventure. It was all so beautiful! Like Rapunzel, princesses-in-training should appreciate and respect the world around them.

How to Treat Your World Like a Princess

✦ Recycle, recycle, recycle!

✦ Find new uses for old items, like Ariel does!

✦ Use both sides of a piece of paper.

✦ Turn the water off when you're not using it.

✦ Don't litter.

✦ Turn the light off when you leave a room.

✦ Plant a garden and take care of it as it grows!

Royal Treatment

Training to be a princess can be exhausting! Even the Disney Princesses need a break every once in a while. Once your noble duties are done, take a little time off to give yourself some well-deserved rest and relaxation.

How to Relax Like a Princess

✦ Take a warm bath.

✦ Smell some fresh flowers.

✦ Curl up with a good book.

✦ Write down your thoughts in a journal or diary.

✦ Take ten slow, even breaths.

✦ Drink a cup of herbal tea or hot cocoa.

✦ Stretch your body from head to toe.

✦ Look up at the sky and watch the clouds go by.

The Right Attitude

The life of a princess isn't always perfect, but it's helpful to stay cheerful and always look on the bright side. Having a positive outlook makes everything easier and gives you the strength you need to turn things around!

How to Stay Positive Like a Princess

✦ Know that everyone has a bad day once in a while—and that's okay!

✦ Keep your sense of humor no matter what.

✦ Be optimistic like Ariel—positive attitudes are contagious!

✦ Think about all the good things in your life.

✦ Remember that even princesses make mistakes!

✦ Sing a favorite song to cheer yourself up.

✦ Talk about your feelings—don't keep them to yourself.

✦ Share a smile with someone you love.

✦ Don't forget: sometimes all you need is a hug!

Follow Your Heart

Princesses always reach for the stars! Tiana often dreamed about owning her own restaurant, but it took hard work and planning to make her dream a reality. If you believe in yourself and follow your heart, your dreams will come true, too!

How to Make Your Dreams Come True Like a Princess

✦ Spend time thinking about what makes you happy.

✦ Trust your heart to guide the way.

✦ Remember that no dream is too big or too small.

✦ Ask for advice from your parents and teachers.

✦ Don't be scared to try something new!

✦ Challenge yourself to be the best you can be!

✦ When you've reached your goals, make new ones.

✦ Be proud of yourself for all you have done!

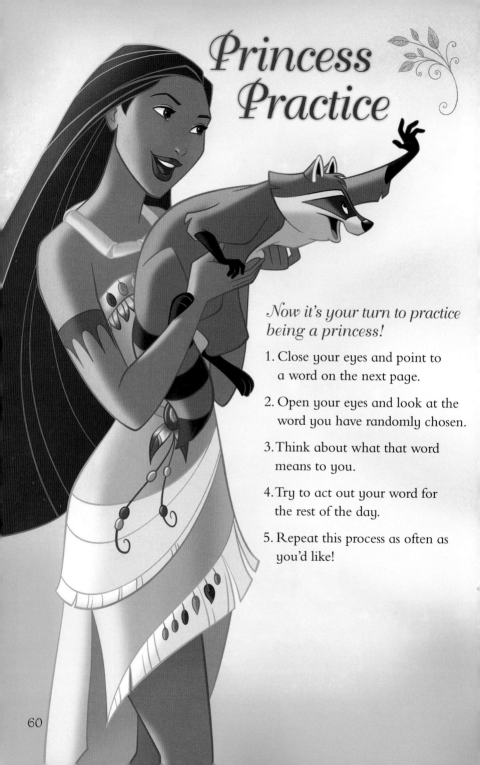

Princess Practice

Now it's your turn to practice being a princess!

1. Close your eyes and point to a word on the next page.

2. Open your eyes and look at the word you have randomly chosen.

3. Think about what that word means to you.

4. Try to act out your word for the rest of the day.

5. Repeat this process as often as you'd like!

Congratulations!

You're officially a princess!

Now it's up to you to make
all your dreams come true!